Happy Easter!

Liesbet Slegers

Clavis

NEW YORK

It's springtime! It's almost Easter!

The sun is shining. The air is warm.

New leaves grow on the trees

and flowers rise from the soil.

Many baby animals are born in the spring.

Birds chirp happily to welcome their babies.

Sheep say BAAA to their newborn lambs.

And Mama chicken is proud of her little chicks.

At school, children make crafts to celebrate
Easter, which will be coming very soon.
They decorate eggs and draw the Easter Bunny.
But, who exactly is the Easter Bunny?

Away in the woods is a little house.

That's where the Easter Bunny lives,

in the middle of a clearing.

As spring begins and Easter approaches,

a very busy period starts for the Easter Bunny!

First, he gathers lots of eggs

from the chickens in their coop.

The chickens are happy to help.

The Easter Bunny fills his basket to the brim.

Back in his house, he gets to work.

He paints the eggs in cheerful colors,

lets them dry, and puts a ribbon around some of them.

It's a big job, but he loves doing it!

Early on Easter morning, the Easter Bunny hops

to the childrens' houses.

His basket is full of eggs:

painted eggs, eggs with ribbons, and lots of chocolate eggs.

He knows children like those the best.

The Easter Bunny hides the eggs all over the place.

He loves hiding eggs so that later, when the children

wake up, they will go on a big Easter egg hunt.

That is always so much fun!

As soon as the children awake, they squeal with delight!

Quickly, they run outside to search for Easter eggs.

They search in, out, under, over, up and down!

Will they find all the Easter eggs?

Easter is a special holiday.

Everyone dresses in their best

colorful spring outfits.

Even the dog wears a bright bow on her head.

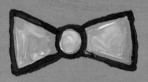

The Easter Bunny has finished his work for the year.

Very tired, he hops back to his little house in the woods

and into his snug, cozy bed for a long, long sleep.

Sleep tight, Easter Bunny! We'll see you next spring!

First published in Belgium and Holland by Clavis Uitgeverij, Hasselt — Amsterdam, 2005
Copyright © 2005, Clavis Uitgeverij

English translation from the Dutch by Clavis Publishing Inc. New York
Copyright © 2012 for the English language edition: Clavis Publishing Inc. New York

Visit us on the web at www.clavisbooks.com

Happy Easter! written and illustrated by Liesbet Slegers
Original title: Piep, het is Pasen!
Translated from the Dutch by Clavis Publishing
English language edition edited by Emma D. Dryden, drydenbks llc

ISBN 978-1-60537-114-6

This book was printed in December 2011 at Proost,
Everdongenlaan 23, B-2300 Turnhout, Belgium

First Edition
10 9 8 7 6 5 4 3 2 1

E SLEGE   ACR
Slegers, Liesbet.
Happy Easter! /

ACRES HOMES
11/13